Published in the United States of America by The Child's World®
1980 Lookout Drive • Mankato, MN 56003-1705
800-599-READ • www.childsworld.com

ACKNOWLEDGMENTS
The Child's World®: Mary Berendes, Publishing Director
The Design Lab: Kathleen Petelinsek, Design and Page Production
Literacy Consultants: Cecilia Minden, PhD, and Joanne Meier, PhD

LIBRARY OF CONGRESS
CATALOGING-IN-PUBLICATION DATA
Moncure, Jane Belk.
 My "t" sound box / by Jane Belk Moncure ; illustrated by
Rebecca Thornburgh.
   p. cm. — (Sound box books)
 Summary: "Little t has an adventure with items beginning with
his letter's sound, such as a toad, two turtles, and a tiger with
tooth troubles."—Provided by publisher.
 ISBN 978-1-60253-160-4 (library bound : alk. paper)
 [1. Alphabet.] I. Thornburgh, Rebecca McKillip, ill. II. Title. III.
Series.

 PZ7.M739Myt 2009
 [E]—dc22   2008033176

A NOTE TO PARENTS AND EDUCATORS:

Magic moon machines and five fat frogs are just a few of the fun things you can share with children by reading books with them. Reading aloud helps children in so many ways! It introduces them to new words, motivates them to develop their own reading skills, and expands their attention span and listening abilities. So it's important to find time each day to share a book or two . . . or three!

As you read with young children, you can help develop their understanding of how print works by talking about the parts of the book—the cover, the title, the illustrations, and the words that tell the story. As you read, use your finger to point to each word, modeling a gentle sweep from left to right.

Simple word games help develop important prereading skills, including an understanding of rhyme and alliteration (when words share the same beginning sound, such as "six" and "sand"). Try playing with words from a book you've just shared: "What other words start with the same sound as moon?" "Cat and hat, do those words rhyme?" The possibilities are endless—and so are the rewards!

My "t" Sound Box®

(Blends are included in this book.)

WRITTEN BY JANE BELK MONCURE

ILLUSTRATED BY REBECCA THORNBURGH

Little  had a box. "I will find things that begin with my † sound," he said. "I will put them into my sound box."

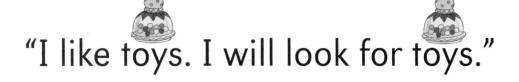

"I like toys. I will look for toys."

Little 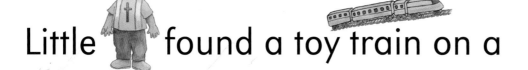 found a toy train on a

train track. Did he put the toy

train and the track into his box?

He did.

Little  found a toy tractor. Did he put the tractor into the box with the toy train and the track?

He did.

Then Little found a truck.

He drove the truck up, up, up

a tall mountain. He drove to the

top, the very tip-top!

At the top of the tall mountain, he

found two turtles. Did he put the

two turtles into his box? He did.

Then he found a toad. Did he put

the toad into the box? He did.

Now the box was so full that

he could not see over the top.

He tripped!

He tumbled down, down, down

the mountain.

He tumbled into a turkey. Turkey

feathers flew!

So Little  made a turkey-

feather hat.

He and the turkey tap-danced

together.

Little 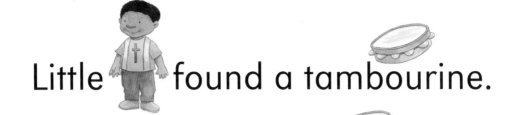 found a tambourine.

He tapped the tambourine. Tap,

tap, tap. Tap, tap, tap.

Little , the turkey, and the

toad tap-danced some more.

Then Little  put all of his

things into the box.

Suddenly, Little  heard a

terrific noise! He ran into a tent.

When he looked out, he saw
a tiger!

The tiger opened its mouth. The tiger's mouth had many teeth.

"I have a loose tooth," said the tiger. "Please pull out my tooth."

So Little  pulled out the tooth.

"Thank you," said the tiger.

Then Little  and the tiger went

inside the tent. They played with

all the toys in the box.

They had a terrific time!

Little 's Word List

tambourine

teeth

tent

tiger

toad

toy

track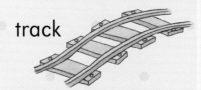

tractor

train

truck

turkey

turtle

Other Words with Little

table

taco

tape

taxi

teapot

telephone

television

tie

tire

tomato

toothbrush

tornado

tray

tree

tuba

More to Do!

You can trace your hands and feet to make silly turkeys!
Ask a friend to help with the tracing.

What you need:

- brown construction paper
- red, yellow, and orange construction paper
- markers

Directions:

1. First, take off your shoes and have your helper trace your feet on the brown paper. Then cut out your foot shapes.

2. Glue the two shapes together at the heels as they are shown in the picture. Be sure not to glue the toes together! These brown shapes will be the turkey's body.

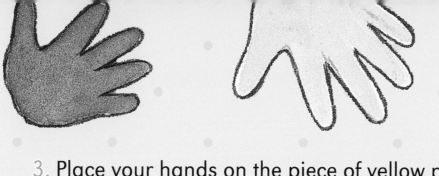

3. Place your hands on the piece of yellow paper. Be sure to spread your fingers out! Ask your helper to trace all around your hands and fingers. Do the same thing on the red and orange pieces of paper. Now cut out your hand shapes.

4. Glue the hands to the back of the brown foot shapes. The hand shapes make the feathers!

5. Draw two eyes and a beak on the brown paper. Now your turkey is finished!

About the Author

Best-selling author Jane Belk Moncure has written over 300 books throughout her teaching and writing career. After earning a Master's degree in Early Childhood Education from Columbia University, she became one of the pioneers in that field. In 1956, she helped form the Virginia Association for Early Childhood Education, which established the first statewide standards for teachers of young children.

Inspired by her work in the classroom, Mrs. Moncure's books have become standards in primary education, and her name is recognized across the country. Her success is reflected not only in her books' popularity with parents, children, and educators, but also by numerous awards, including the 1984 C. S. Lewis Gold Medal Award.

About the Illustrator

Rebecca Thornburgh lives in a pleasantly spooky old house in Philadelphia. If she's not at her drawing table, she's reading—or singing with her band, called Reckless Amateurs. Rebecca has one husband, two daughters, and two silly dogs.